My Saturdays with Grumps

Peter Cook-Jones

ISBN: 9798840682845

DEDICATION

To all those that have
fond memories of their childhood, and especially if they have shared precious moments with an older member of the family.

CONTENTS

ACKNOWLEDGMENTS

These stories were inspired by the writings of
Bates, Hardy, Doyle and Dickens.

INTRODUCTION

This is a collection of ten stories about my relationship with my grandfather, whom I called 'Grumps'.

He was an extraordinary man, a larger-than-life figure who never failed to amuse and delight.

He'd seen many changes in his long life, but somehow remained unchanged himself.

Grumps was happiest when cultivating his beloved garden, where he grew magnificent specimens of beans, potatoes and damsons (to make wine), and the biggest, healthiest looking pumpkins I'd ever seen, and these he gave away to local children for Halloween night.

Any prize-winning vegetables that were not eaten were donated to charity.

Grumps had done everything and had been everywhere, or so he would have you believe.

He never actually said those words, but that's the impression that I got from listening to his stories, tales that he told me over the years.

I called him Grumps, not because he was Grumpy, although he could be at times. It was due to me not being able to say grandpa when I was a toddler.

It always came out as Grumps and the name stuck.

Over the years and right up to his death, my visits had allowed him to recall his life's experiences and adventures.

I was as eager to listen as he was to talk.

We were similar in character, both liking the outdoor life and being what he called 'left of centre,' although I came to understand that later in life.

Grumps had a way of talking that was very amusing, often animatedly using his hands and pulling funny faces.

Some stories were told when my grandmother was in the same room, when it was too wet or cold to go to his shed, or den, as he liked to call it.

She would sit behind him, knitting or reading, and give me clues to the accuracy of the tales.

A raised eyebrow or a purse of her lips was often enough to tell if he was kidding me.

Mostly, they were authentic and truthful stories with just a slight stretching of the truth on occasions.

He, of course, was not aware that she was even listening, thinking her to be almost deaf, but she had selective hearing, which I have noticed in some people. Occasionally she would tell him off with "Now, don't be filling the lad's head with a lot of nonsense." But it did not deter him.

1.
Grumps and the owl

On one warm spring Saturday evening, I went to visit my grandfather after a spell of absence.

It was at the weekends, and more usually on a Saturday when I would spend time with him, but I had been unwell with a cold for ten days and had not wanted him to come down with it.

Pushing through the matted brambles that were now covering the garden path, I found him in his den at the end of the garden.

It was looking a bit run down, and I offered to spruce it up a bit in the holidays for him.

"Spruce it up! What's wrong with it?" he huffed. He was adamant that it was fine as it was.

"Thank you very much,

"How long have you been coming down here, talking about how you would get those brambles sorted?" I joked.

He replied.

"Oh, I forget exactly, anyway, don't matter at my time o' life, I always manage to get through to my refuge, my den. Do you know, I built it before you were born lad? And many stories it would tell if it could talk, yes, many stories." He said, patting the timbers as if they were an old friend. Then he added.

"Anyway, you've got enough to do with your college work to worry about my shed, although a bit of help with the garden would be nice."

"Don't worry, I'll have a go at the brambles next weekend," I told him, not thinking that they keep on growing, and I would probably have a job for life.

"Do you remember coming here as a youngster?" he said, gazing out of the cobweb-covered window with a faraway look.

"I remember, and do you recall I thought then that it was only children that had dens?"

Grumps let out a huge laugh, saying,

"A lot of men when they get married will have a place that they can hide away in, and I have also heard that there are some women that have a room where the husband ain't allowed. Now you're here, how about I tell you about the time I discovered an enormous owl?"

I wanted to know more, of course, and as Grumps loved telling stories, I knew it would be another good one.

Grumps, by this time, was getting quite excited and itching to tell me, so he sat me down in one of the old leather armchairs while he went to get a bottle of his 'old peculiar', a home-made ale brewed to his recipe. Let me say at this point that his den was, in fact, quite comfortable, with a couple of old leather armchairs that smelt of tobacco smoke, a pot-bellied stove on which he would boil an old, blackened kettle.

Then there was a pipe rack full of old, smelly tobacco pipes, that he had collected from around the world. He also had a radio so that he could listen to the news or gardening programmes.

I remember that the roof leaked down one end and the rain would ting, plop and splash into an old paint tin, then on dry days he'd throw it on the garden.

Grumps came back and plonked himself down next to me in the other armchair, dust flying everywhere, I poured out two glasses of beer, and then he told me this tale.

"Well, it was like this," he began with a twinkle in his eye,

"I would come down to the den of an evening, regular like, because of the missus, your gran, being out at her regular bingo sessions or visiting friends. We'd have tea around five, then she would scoot off. She never won very much at bingo, but it was a chance for her to meet up with different people.

I would look forward to these evenings, being able to smoke me pipe and do me model making. You've seen it, the Cutty Sark, the great historical sailing ship," he said proudly pointing to the model on the shelf, but you couldn't miss it as it took pride of place.

I had indeed seen it grow, rising like the Phoenix from a pile of old lolly sticks he would shape and cut, till he had turned out the magnificent scale model it was today.

"And very fine it is too," I chimed in, but I was eager to hear the story.

He went on...

"Well, one Tuesday I went down, as usual, to set about me model making, have a doze and finish preparing me 'omemade beer, like the one you're drinkin' now." He stopped for a breath and another sip. As he started to doze off, I nudged him gently and he sprang back into the story.

"Don't worry, I was just resting my eyes, where was I? Oh yes, give me a minute and I'll tell you the rest."

This time he did nod off for a few minutes and as I sat watching him quietly snoring, I noticed he still had a smile on his face. Maybe the story or perhaps the beer had a hand in that. During those few minutes, a thought came to me.

He had always worn the same clothes every weekend, when I would visit him, first with my parents taking me as a child, and then later in my teens before I left home.

His dark-green corduroy trousers always seemed to be hitched up too high, up from his waist to the bottom of his chest, held up by white braces. Then there was the black waistcoat that he called a weskit, half undone, with a silver watch and chain attached. It made him look important, although the collarless shirt ruined the effect. He wore brown shoes that were polished so much that you could see your reflection in them, and Grumps smoked an old briar pipe that was never out of his mouth even when talking, and he talked a lot.

When he awoke, he signalled for more beer and then resumed his story.

"Well, this one time, a queer thing happened. It was a damp, frosty evening in late November, deathly quiet, with an icy mist that acted as a blanket, muffling the sounds from the streets. I went outside to breathe the fresh chill air and I heard it."

"Heard what?" I asked "Ghosts?" I teased him.

"I heard an owl, very soft, like it was a long way away, but very clear, then after a couple of minutes it stopped, so I went inside and thought no more about it."

"Is that it? Not much of a story, was it?" I grumbled, I was ready to leave,

disappointed, but he knew I was only teasing again.

"No, that was not *it*, I just paused for a breath, so if you want to hear the rest, please sit quietly. I'm coming to the interesting part now."
I wanted to hear the rest, so pulling the armchair closer, I sat forward to listen, then topped up our glasses again just to help him lubricate his lips, you understand, so he could continue.

"We have never had owls down this way before, so hearing this was a real treat for me and wanting to encourage them, I hooted back. Every evening for two weeks after that, down here at the den, the same thing happened: a couple of minutes of hooting, then nothing. I called back, trying to make a decent owl sound, toowitt-toowoo."

My grandfather stopped here to give me a demonstration, comical really, not very convincing, but I kept quiet. It was getting dark outside now and I fancied I could see a shadow of an owl in the tree just outside the dusty window. Demonstration over, he went on.

"I thought I might get the creature to come to me. I had even been putting food out for it."
"What sort of food, do you know what owls eat?"
"Oh, I put a few nuts, seeds, and a saucer of water."

"Then, after a couple of minutes, it stopped again, as if it were listening out for my call, but each evening it got louder and louder, and then one time I could swear that it was just on the other side of the hedge. This was going to be an enormous owl, and I was not sure what I would do when I saw it. I could hear leaves and branches quietly rustling. I had to see it, so I moved quietly towards the hedge, parted a few leaves and branches, and there he was, staring me in the face."

"The owl?" I whispered, moving nearer to him.

"The owl? No, not a bloomin' owl, it was a neighbour who had been making owl noises trying to attract owls the same way that I was. With his hands cupped around his mouth right in front of me, he thought that the calling back was a real owl, and he was just as surprised as I was. We had both been calling out to each other, and we suddenly felt stupid."

"Then we fell about laughing and ended up in the brambles, although that part was no laughing matter. However, we promised not to tell our wives for fear of being ridiculed, and you are the first person I have ever told, so Mum's the word, eh, promise?"

Grumps lived to the ripe old age of ninety-nine, and for as long as I live, that story and an image of him, face to face with his neighbour, in amongst the brambles remain with me.

I promised, and up till now, I have kept that promise. It was, after all, a long time ago.

2.
Grumps, the dog whisperer.

During the spring and summer, the longer, warmer, bright days had meant that my grandfather could spend more time in the garden. Grumps was a bit of a celebrity at the local farmers' market, where he would show off his prize-winning vegetables, but during the depths of winter he'd be stuck indoors, and we'd find him at the window grumbling,

"I can't wait to get out there. Do you see that gran? it's getting brighter every day, isn't it? Yes, it won't be long now."

This drama would start on 22nd December after the shortest day, going through that ritual every morning until it was warm and nice enough to get back to gardening again. Then he would be outside all day, every day, and only pop inside his den if it rained.

He was not an indoor person, and it was never *too* hot for him outside. Getting his shirt off and getting stuck in was his way.

I also longed for those warmer, brighter days when I could go round to help, when the garden was lush, brimming with brassicas, and a cherry tree that would shed a carpet of pink blossom, white butterflies would visit, and he would try hard to keep them away from the plants, but they always found a way in.

Then as the year went on, he'd have runner beans on tall canes, potatoes, and not forgetting the lovely colourful flower borders.

I helped on Saturdays, trying to keep it all tidy, cutting back the brambles that seemed to be determined to strangle everything, and to keep him company.

He liked nothing more than to chat, and in between bouts of planting and weeding, he would usher me into the den, take up his pipe and tobacco, pour some 'ome-made beer or wine, and tell me stories. Some were silly, while others were quite poignant or uplifting, but each one revealed different aspects of his character and his colourful life.

One Saturday we were sitting and chatting, when an old friend of his turned up at the house. The man was of similar age, maybe a little older, and he'd known Grumps some years before. They'd been out of touch for years, but that day he had tracked Grumps down.

The visitor, Eric, had with him a rather lovely Old English sheepdog, named Sophie, and while the two men sat chatting, Sophie just slept. Grumps introduced me to Eric, and I listened to the conversation with interest, as it revealed something of Grumps' past.

It turned out that they had worked together as keen gardeners back when they were younger, and then Eric had wanted to move to France, but Grumps stayed in the UK.

They talked about some of the places they had visited together some years previously, comparing notes about the ones that they'd been to, and all the while, the dog lay there sleeping.

Grumps asked about Sophie. Was she related to one that Eric had owned many years ago? A dog that Grumps remembered, and by the sound of it, and knew very well. Eric told him that she was a descendant of Betty, whom Grumps had looked after for Eric some time ago.

After chatting for an hour, Eric had to leave, but they had promised to keep in touch one way or another. Eric was going back to France so they would have to communicate by email. Grumps, of course, knew about email, but he did not own a computer and was unlikely to get one. I offered to help by using my account and be a go-between.

As he was leaving, Eric said to Grumps,

"Tell the lad about Betty and the wine."

Chuckling as he walked away. Eric went off with Sophie and I never saw them again. Grumps turned to me and said,

"Time for a bit more gardening, eh, lad? We can stop a bit later for that story, with drinks and baccy."

So, we got stuck in, me weeding and clearing, Grumps preparing the ground to plant something new.

After about an hour, Grumps stopped digging and said to me,

"Queer thing that, Eric just popping up out of the blue like that, when I last saw him, I was in France, before I met your gran, many years ago. I had looked after his dog, the grandparent of Sophie. I bumped into him quite by accident. That was a bit of a lark, I can tell you. I didn't expect to see him again, not after what happened."

Eric's parting comment intrigued me then, and I wanted to know more, so I asked him to tell me about it.

"C'mon then, let's go to the den. I'm getting thirsty and I might even get the pipe and baccy out." He said with a laugh.

Once settled, and pipe lit, I poured the drinks, then he told me, in his inimitable way.

"Many years ago," he began, "I went to France with a close friend, Mark. We were going on a cycling and camping holiday. Another mate, Jim, took us over on the night ferry from Portsmouth in his car, carrying our bikes on the roof rack. Then he'd return to Portsmouth, leaving us to it. So, we cycled off, camping some nights and taking a Chambre de Hôte, occasionally, to get cleaned up."

"Chambre de what?" I asked.

"Chambre de Hôte, it's a room with breakfast, usually in a farmhouse, where the owners live. They'd put you up for the night, for a few Francs as it was back then, you know before the Euro came in?"

"Like a B & B here in the UK." I asked.

"Exactly, you've got it." he replied.

"I was a keen cyclist back then, but we made the mistake of mixing cycling with camping. It was quite challenging, carrying everything and packing it all away each time. But we managed it, and a bit of friendly rivalry helped the trip along."

"How far did you go, and for how long?" I asked him.

"We went away with no fixed time in mind and cycled around the Loire Valley, stopping for one or two nights at a time. We had a wonderful trip, but we also had a couple of not so funny experiences," I asked him to tell me all the good and bad stuff.

Grumps continued.

"For example, when we arrived in St Malo, on the North coast, it was early in the morning, about seven o'clock, and we were ready for our breakfast, so we looked for a café. Well, there was not much open, except a couple of bakeries, but we wanted something more filling, and hot if we could get it.

Then, a few kilometres down the road, we found a place that was open, and we agreed that this looked ideal."

"With high expectations we went in, but they were soon to be dashed when we saw the state of the place."

Grumps stopped talking to tap out his burnt tobacco and fill up his pipe, the stale old ash didn't smell so good, but within seconds the rich aroma had filled the air, now he had a satisfied look on his face, and I prompted him again to tell all, so he started up again.

"I must say that neither of us could speak French, and the owner did not speak any English, and why would he? In rural France, they did not need to, so we had to make ourselves understood the best we could."

"He was a grubby-looking man, wearing a dirty vest that would have been white when had first bought it, and he had a cigarette in the corner of his mouth, dropping ash everywhere.

We started with 'Bonjour', that much we knew, and then asked for eggs, and he looked at us as if we were mad. Shrugging his shoulders, he obviously did not get it. So, we tried saying it with a French accent, but he wasn't having any of it. I tried 'cock-a-doodle-doo,' and Mark pointed out that I was making a cockerel noise, not a hen, and just as I was about to flap my arms up and down and cluck, the owner got the message."

'Ah, Bon!' was all he said, disappearing into the kitchen.

"We looked at each other and questioned whether we wanted to stay or run, but then he came back with plates, and on each plate were two fried eggs, floating in a sea of oil. We were not impressed."

"Just eggs, nothing else, no toast or bread?" I asked.

"Nothing but eggs, and when I asked for toast, he said, 'tost, huh!' shrugged his greasy shoulders and walked away. Trying to eat fried eggs with a fork is difficult, and without bread or toast, it was impossible.

We left there hungry, having declined the floating eggs, and made for our first camp stop, picking up provisions on the way."

"Ok," I said, "so you got off to a rotten start. Did things settle down after that?"

"No," Grumps sighed. "The next day, Mark went to have a shower and as he reached for his glasses, he knocked them onto the hard tiled floor and broke a lens, and without them he could see very little.

We were stuck out in the sticks with no optician for miles.

I told him I would lead the way and he should cycle with his front wheel close to my back wheel for guidance, and we went off around the junk shops looking for used glasses, raking through old leather cases that were filled with them. We cycled like this for hours, trying all of them, highly dangerous, but we had to do it, although we found nothing suitable."

"We eventually came to the town of Brissac and found an optician open. You'd have thought we had struck gold the way we jumped for joy,"

"Great! So, you got that sorted out then?" I asked.

"No, you'd have thought so, but although the optician could do 'same day' repairs allegedly, he messed up, and made a new lens the same as the unbroken lens, and of course, people's eyes are not the same on both sides. It was all wrong, and Mark could still only see out of one eye."

"Unfortunately, the optician swapped the lenses around, thinking that was the problem, so now he couldn't see straight out of either of 'em. It was getting late by this time, but we persuaded him to do a full eye test and make a new pair of glasses. We had to come back the next day for them, but Mark got fixed up and was not charged for the glasses or the eye test, as a sort of apology."

"By then, the money was drying up. Mark had the idea of looking for casual work, and after scouring the notice boards we saw an advert in English, which read; URGENT, House (and dog) sitter needed, English resident going to the UK for six weeks. Come and ask for Eric."

"I thought, 'surely that can't be the Eric I knew back in England.' I knew he'd moved to that area, but how strange that would be."

Grumps grinned and said, "We walked to the house that was advertised, which was about ten minutes away, knocked on the door, and Eric, who you just saw, answered it."

"Wow, that was a stroke of luck Grumps. Did you get the job?" I asked.

"Yes, we did. After standing for a second or two, hardly believing our eyes, Eric invited us in and explained what he needed. We chatted about gardening and the old days, and how he came to be there, working for a travel company.

However, he had to go back to England for six weeks and needed someone to stay in the house, to keep it safe and look after Betty, his beloved dog. It couldn't have worked out better, or so we thought, but things changed as time went on."

"We only just caught Eric in time as he was going off the next day, and that would have meant putting the dog into kennels and seeing as he would be away for six weeks, Betty would have hated it. Eric was so happy to see us, and we were looking forward to staying there."

Grumps stopped talking to re-fill with tobacco. He also made a gesture for me to re-fill the glasses. I couldn't help asking Grumps,

"What on earth were you thinking about? I thought you didn't like dogs?"

"Yes, well, that's true," Grumps replied, "to a certain extent, but if that was what it took to get free accommodation, then so be it. We asked to see the dog and wanted to know if there was anything special, we had to do, or know about before we agreed to stay there and take on the responsibility." Eric called out, 'Bett-eeee! Bett-eeee! come here girl,' and this huge Old English sheepdog called Betty came bounding up and nearly knocked us over. Eric told us,

'She can be a bit excitable, but she's no trouble and a big softy, really.'

"After she had calmed down a bit, Eric gave us a long list of rules and instructions for us to take care of, saying."

"Follow this guide to the letter and you won't have any problems. It's a strict regime she's on, it's all there, have a read while I pack, say hello to Betty."

Grumps handed me a piece of crumpled up paper that he'd kept for years, saving it as a memento. It was a list of all the things to do, to follow and to watch out for.

This is how it read:

**6.30 in the morning, put her outside, for 10 min's, don't let her get too hot, call her back in, and give her a water bowl*

**Give one handful of dried biscuits, mixed with half a tin of corned beef.*

**Keep her in until the postie has been, DO NOT LET HER CHASE THE POSTIE*

**Let her out for 15 mins exercise, be careful of the heat, no trampling the veg patch*

**Call her, especially, like this; Bett-eeee! using a long 'e' sound, rising sharply*

**She sleeps around 10.00, in the bathroom where it's cooler, shut the door she snores.*

**Let her out at 12.00, 10 mins, and follow rule one again*

.

**Give another handful of dried biscuits and the other half of the corned beef.*

**When you take her out on the lead, make sure she does not bump into things as she is very short-sighted.*
She knows her way around the house, so don't re-arrange the furniture.

**For any illness or accident, we have an account with the local vet, and you'll find his number is on the notice board.*

** Don't sit in her chair (the big comfy armchair) she will sulk and refuse food.*

**She can't jump into a car so you would have to carry her (she weighs 50 kg!)*

**Have fun, my UK telephone number is also on the notice board.*

Grumps asked me,
"What do you think of that, me boyo, a neurotic dog with a neurotic owner, or what?"
I was shocked, then I fell about laughing, nearly choking on my drink, then said,
"Six weeks of that nonsense, all those rules and regulations. I bet you didn't stick to them closely,

did you? C'mon, be honest?"

Grumps then told me what they really did.

"Well, it started ok, but we were on holiday, so the idea of getting up at 6.30 was out of order. We left the door open so Betty could choose when to come and go, and she seemed happy with that. She would come in when it got hot, as any creature would."

"Sounds reasonable," I said.

"Of course, that meant she might be out in the garden when the postie called, but he always put the mail in the post-box at the gate when he saw her out, and it gave Betty a bit of exercise chasing after him."

"Then our money ran out, and we had to wait for a cheque from home. Despite having all the vegetables in the garden, we thought that something a bit more substantial would go down better. Mark suggested eating the corned beef. There were dozens of tins in the cupboard, so we supplemented our diet with corned beef, and gave Betty some more biscuits to compensate. Then we used spinach and other vegetables to make up recipes based around those tins of meat, it wasn't dog food, it was the regular human stuff you buy at the supermarket, and Betty seemed to be ok about it, and it stopped her poo-ing so much."

Grumps made me laugh, and I had a picture in my mind of this dog and those two for ages afterwards. It was so crazy. I topped up the home brew, and he started up again.

"Then there was the thing about Betty bumping into things. Eric was sure that it was because of old age, but I had a different idea. You've seen the pictures of Old English sheepdogs, I suppose?" Grumps asked.

"Oh yes, lots of hair, and a lot of it hanging over the dog's eyes," I replied.

"That's right, me lad, over the eyes, and what do you think would happen if you had hair over your eyes?" He asked, with a big grin on his face.

"I suppose I wouldn't be able to see anything, or not very well at least," I told him.

"Exactly!" Grumps clapped his hands together loudly,

"So wouldn't that be the same for the dog?" he suggested.

"You didn't?... you can't have done?" I stammered.

"I did. I cut the fringe so that she could see better, and old Betty sprung into life, she could see! She stopped bumping into the furniture and even went galloping about the garden. This was a new dog. Things were a lot easier from then on for the three of us," Grumps laughed.

I asked,

"Didn't Eric say anything when he got back?"

"He did, but I told a bit of a porky, saying that Betty had got a load of those sticky grass balls matted into her hair. You know, the ones found in long grass?

Well, I had to cut them out, "I was only thinking of her comfort," I told him."

"The next drama came when Betty developed an abscess on her under-belly. It was getting bigger by the day, and it ended up the size of a tennis ball, and we thought the dog would die. Betty wouldn't eat or get up off her bed, we did the right thing and called the vet, who told us to, 'Bring her in,' which was all very well for him to say, but a fifty-kilo sick dog would not be easy to shift."

"How did you do it?" I was keen to know.

"Sheer hard work, me lad, and a bit of clever thinking. We made a sled, a sort of sliding affair made with ropes, her bed, and some cardboard we found in the cellar. The dog lay on her bed, and then we slipped the cardboard underneath, tied a bit of rope to it, and hauled it up the path. Nearing the top, Mark collapsed in a heap, so we rang the vet and he said he would come to us, and 'not to worry,' after all that puffing and panting, we were worried that she would die. We had been trusted to look after the dog, not kill it.

The vet lanced the abscess, and Betty slowly recovered over the following week, and seemed to be bouncier than before, which was not surprising I suppose, happy to be well again."

"All that, while you were trying to have a holiday," I said, "sounds like you'd have been glad to get home for a break?" I joked.

Grumps hadn't finished and continued the tale of woe with this parting shot.

"Before we could come back, and don't forget Eric was away for weeks, we had one last thing to do."

"Go on then, Grumps, let's hear it. I hope the house was still standing." I quipped.

"Yes, no worries on that front, but we thought we should replace all the wine we had been drinking from the cellar. Don't forget that we had very little money when we first went there."

"I was still waiting for a cheque from home, but that took a while back in those days, so we thought that we'd drink the wine and replace it when the money came through and no one would be any wiser or out of pocket."

"And did it come through?" I asked, imagining another problem.

"It did, so we took the last bottle with its label around to all the shops and vineyards to show which wine we were looking for. Would you believe it?

That one was no longer available, they could sell us this or that wine, but not the same as we'd drank. Panic set in as we tried every outlet. We were at it for days, even tried the supermarkets, but we failed miserably."

I asked him.

"What happened? Did you get into trouble?"

"When Eric got back, we talked about the house and the dog, the garden, the weather, and I was waiting for him to notice the wine, or lack of wine, which he did eventually."

"Oh, dear!" I exclaimed, "had you'd been caught out?"

Grumps smiled and said,

"That's what we'd thought at first, but Eric asked if we had enjoyed the wine and we sheepishly said yes, but we had tried everything and everywhere to replace it, and we were sorry to say that we couldn't find the same make.

"Eric roared with laughter, and said,

"That wine was for you. I left it as a thank you for looking after everything. Didn't you see the note that I left you? So, there's no need to replace anything. You've spent hours searching for what was my gift to you."

"That was the six weeks finished. When it was time to leave, what do you think Mark found in one

of his saddlebags?" Grumps asked.
I said that couldn't even imagine.
"A bloomin' spare pair of glasses that he had forgotten from an earlier trip! I could have murdered him!"
Grumps admitted to me then that he'd felt foolish, and tired, which is not something he would say often.

3.
Grumps and the Burmese Tiger

My grandpa Grumps had retired from working before I was born, so I only knew him and my grandma as elderly, but despite the age and generation gap we were good together.

Grumps would tell me stories while my father was away in the Merchant Navy, he had someone to share his stories with. He would talk and I would listen and ask more questions, it was a good arrangement.

Around the middle of July, during a very hot spell of weather, I went to see Grumps on one of my regular Saturday visits.

While we worked in the garden, I brought up the subject of my leaving school. We discussed my future work options now that I had finished my exams, and I told him I had made no decisions and was still waiting for my exam results; maybe I should go to college before looking for work, and could he give me some ideas. I asked him about his younger days at work, before retirement, what had he done, what had been his profession, had he enjoyed his working life?

Grumps was never hasty when answering my questions. Instead, he would fill a pipe with one of his aromatic tobaccos, pour us some homebrew, pause a bit, and then he would answer me.

It is fair to say that his home brew was never very strong, and I had been drinking with him since I was about twelve.

This time was no different, so I sat back in one of his deep old leather armchairs in his den, grateful for a break, and waited patiently for him to begin.

"Now there's a question, what I have never done would be easier to answer, (Grumps was prone to exaggeration), but as for my job or profession, well, that's different." He took a puff on his pipe, had a mouthful of brew, and told me of his younger days.

"First job I had was a Saturday job in my last year of school, where I worked in a hardware shop selling timber, tools, and paint, it didn't last long because the boss sacked me because of an 'incident' with a customer."

"What do you mean by an 'incident'? Did you upset someone?" I asked.

"Hold your horses, I am coming to it. I was young and brash, and a customer asked for a certain make of paint, one which had been discontinued. So, eager to please, I went out back to the store to check. Maybe there was a tin that had been overlooked."

"Well, funny enough, I found one."

"It really must have been the last one and showed it to the customer. This delighted him, until I suggested he should pay double as it was such a rare tin, a 'collectors' piece,' of course I was teasing him.

"Oh Grumps, that was a bit wicked, wasn't it, what did he do?" I asked.

"He stormed out of the shop, not realising that I was only messing about, but he made a complaint and that was the end of that job. Well, not quite the end because the owner had to go away for a couple of days, and although he had a 'second in command', the shop needed two people, one in front and one out the back, cutting timber. So, I accepted his offer of double pay for those days and turned up as required."

"It sounds like you were a bit of a mercenary," I suggested.

"I needed the money, yes, if that's what you mean?" He replied.

Grumps went on,

"There was one customer who had been a regular customer, she was very fussy and wanted everything done for her. She would come in with a drawing scratched out on a scrap of paper, asking, 'Could you make this for me?' it may have been a bird house or something, anyway she was very demanding. One time she came in asking for several pieces of timber cut to a certain length, and Paul, the other chap, explained that it would have to be later as he was busy. He gave her two-metre lengths to cut up herself at home. She was not happy but bought them anyway.

Then Paul sent her out with the long lengths onto the street. But the busy road defeated her, as every time she tried to cross, the cars sped by from both directions, leaving her spinning around on the central reservation like a 'whirling dervish', for a minute or two we found it funny, but I took pity and rescued her and got her to the other side."

"I left after that, and I got myself an apprenticeship working with wood. I became a cabinetmaker and worked with wood the rest of my days."

I was eager to know what he had made over the years, perhaps some of the furniture in his house, or my parent's house. Grumps was just as eager to tell me.

"Oh, I made fitted wardrobes in ours and your house, our big dining table, and I even made the polished hardwood stairs you can see in our hallway."

"Wow! I never knew that you made those stairs that must have been a complicated job." I was now in awe of my grandfather and wanted to know more.

"I have plenty of stories of when I was an apprentice, but they can keep for another time.

After I finished my five-year apprenticeship, I rented a small workshop and started working on my own, stair making was my speciality. Anyway, I'm coming to the funny part."

"What could be funny about making stairs?" I asked.

"It was not the making that was funny, it was the fitting. I had a very awkward customer one time, and the fuss he made, and the scene that followed was hilarious."

Grumps stopped for more beer and baccy before continuing.

"Well, I called this customer the 'Burmese Tiger' on account of his fiery temper and unpredictable nature.

He had worked in Burma in the Diplomatic Corp, although I never found him very diplomatic with me. Predictably, we had a falling out.

I had made him a flight of stairs and arranged to take them at 9 o'clock one morning; he had specifically asked that it was not to be before 9 am. When I asked why, he told me he had to get his things up to his office before I arrived, and then he could work there while I was fitting the stairs.

I arrived a bit early with a mate called Scotty, who was to help me fit the big old stairs. He knocked on the door at about 8.45 and the 'Tigers' wife answered it, and in the background, we could hear 'The Burmese Tiger' shouting; 'Tell them to *GO*

AWAY! and come back at 9 am as we had arranged.'

"Scotty was fuming. He was very quick to get annoyed, and wanted to duff the client up, but I told him to calm down and we would take our time. We'd drink from our flasks and go when *we* were ready."

"We eventually got the staircase in the house by about 9.15 and he was still shrieking at us."

"Did you end up in a fight? did Scotty have a go at him?" I was eager to know.

"No, we carried on and ignored him. That made him more furious and when it came to fixing the stairs in place, I made an enormous error. He did not tell me that there were water pipes in the space under the floor, and I drilled a hole to fix the newel post and hit a water pipe."

"Oh Grumps, you didn't, seriously? What on earth did you do then?" I asked, shocked.

"I put the drill back in the hole."

"Just like the boy who put his finger in the dike. I remember that from school."

"Yes, a bit like that, but the floor was under water by then, and the 'Tiger' was not a happy bunny, as they say."

I couldn't resist and said.

"I don't suppose he was a happy Tiger? either," Grumps thought that was funny.

"He was furious and beside himself with rage, and

shouting," *'DO SOMETHING ABOUT IT!' and 'GET A PLUMBER!'.*

"Unfortunately, he lived in a three-story house, with a lot of pipework, so I told him to turn off any stop taps that came into the property and turn on all the basin taps to empty the pipes while I called the plumber."

"Now all this happened in a little village where there were not dozens of plumbers to choose from, and the only one available was busy with another job."

"When I rang him, he told me he would be a little while and would get there as quickly as he could. I explained the situation and the plumber, Ron, thought it was hilarious, as he had previously dealt with this chap before."

The problem was that the 'Tiger' had been downright rude and had then asked for a discount. Ron was not feeling warm toward him."

"I told the client he was next on the list, and of course, that wasn't good enough for him, but he had no choice. At least we had got the water to slow down but it seeped under the hardwood floor."

"When the plumber came into the house, the Burmese Tiger shouted at him."

'HURRY UP, GET A MOVE ON!

'This made Ron laugh, and the more he laughed, the 'Tiger' got more agitated. So, you get the picture?" Grumps asked.

"There's a man beside himself with rage looking down at us, he's stuck up on the next floor, and Ron was looking at him in disbelief saying,

"I am the one who has the tools and the know-how to fix this, so I suggest you stop your shouting, and behaving like a spoilt child, or you will be upstairs for a long time."

Ron then rolled a cigarette, slowly, and waited till he'd calmed down. Then he asked the Tiger, "What's your occupation?" "Ron knew really, he was just trying to wind him up. To which the Tiger replied,"

"I am a retired Civil Servant, in the Diplomatic Corps, in Burma as it was called back then. Why?"

Ron shouted back up the stairwell,

"Well, really? you're not being very diplomatic here, are you? We are not some of your little slave boys that you are used to bullying and threatening. Just shut up and we will fix this."

The furious client shouted down,

"Nobody will get paid until this gets sorted out."

"Then a shower of dust came floating down as he stamped his feet in what I can only describe as a tantrum, or 'hissy fit' as you young uns might say." Ron replied.

"No way, we will want to be paid before we do the job, both of us, as I have no confidence in ever getting the money from you."

"Then the owner had to get his wife, who was downstairs, to hand over a cheque before we did any more work because we were certain that he would not have paid us."

"How did it end?" I asked Grumps,

"Did you get it sorted out without a fight?"

"Yep, we fixed the leak, and I fitted the stairs without another word from him, although we could hear him grumbling to himself way up in the other room. We were lucky, because he was a very nasty man, and I did no more work for him, and Scotty never got the 'punch up', which I think he was secretly looking forward to. And that would have had a whole different outcome, as I still had to work in the area."

4.
The Elephant in the room.

In my grandfather's Den, hanging on the wall, was a most peculiar thing. It was a hat like those worn by Rangers in safari films. The hat itself was not odd but what was it doing in an Englishman's shed?

It had been there for as long as I could remember, and now, covered in dust, it fell off the nail that it was hanging on, and landed in my lap.

I was there visiting Grumps on a Saturday, which had been my habit pretty much every week for most of my teenage years.

He would always have a tale or yarn to tell, and I was always ready to listen because he had a way of making me believe them, even if some of them were really beyond belief.

They'd always start the same way, that is, Grumps could never tell a story without one of his favourite pipes filled with aromatic tobacco, and a glass of 'something' to wet his whistle.

He made extremely good wine from garden vegetables or fruit from his extensive garden. They never tasted of the produce itself, and that was where his skills lay, brewing and refining until it was as good, if not better, than a lot of commercial wines.

Beer was his other hobby, which he called his 'Ome' brew, although these were crafted using shop-bought kits, but were equally delicious.

This day was no different, and fully charged with ale and 'baccy,' he picked up the hat, saying,

"That's handy." Grumps said, "I'd forgotten about this hat. I've a mind to wear it in the garden. It will keep the sun off when I'm digging me spuds." he said, placing it on his head and looking as pleased as punch. Then he placed it on my head where it slid right down over my eyes so that I could see nothing.

"Where on earth did it come from Grumps," I asked. "it's been up there for years, but we've never talked about it. There is usually a silly story behind all your stuff." I said, teasing him.

"Silly! Grumps exclaimed, not bloomin' silly at all. It might be phantasmagorical, but definitely not silly. I've a good mind not to tell you if you think like that.", he was teasing me this time, of course, as he often did.

I quizzed him,

"What's it made of, anyway? There's no weight to it, but it feels like it might resist crushing, say if a monkey dropped something on your head."

Grumps said,

"It's a Pith hat me lad, or a Sola Topa if you are in

a Spanish-speaking country where I believe they originated and designed to keep the sun off of your bonce."

"Bonce?" I queried, "what's that?"

"Your head, and it also allows for a bit of space underneath for the air to move about, keeping you cool. They're made from a substance extracted from cork, mixed with glue, and moulded to that shape.

Come on, it's stuffy in here, let's go out onto the veranda, it's a hot day but there's a bit of air outside, bring the drinks and I'll tell you where and how I got it." We picked up the hat, drinks and his pipe and went out onto the veranda to settle down for a story.

The veranda ran alongside the shed or den as he called it, and although the decking was still solid, the little sloping roof was failing and gave little protection from the sun, so I suggested Grumps put on his Pith hat while I wore an old baseball cap.

There was a small homemade three-legged table to put the drinks on, and a couple of old cane-seated chairs we had to put cushions on to be comfortable. Once we had settled, I pressed him again to tell me about how he got the hat.

"I suppose you're gonna tell me you were in India hunting Tigers or big game?" I suggested.

"India?" Grumps began, "No, not India, no it was

in Africa, m'boyo, Africa on safari."

"Some years ago, I took your gran on a package holiday to Africa. We went to visit the Victoria Falls and then travelled on the Zambezi River to Chobe National Park in Botswana where we would go on Safari."

"Thank goodness for that," I chipped in. "I had visions of you and gran deep in the jungle, with leeches and all those creepy crawlies. Africa, eh? Well, that is not so bad, I suppose."

Grumps chuckled at that, saying,

"Don't you think they have dangerous animals in Africa?"

He was still laughing when he tried to drink his beer and nearly choked on it, so he paused there to re-fill his pipe and regain his composure. I said.

"C'mon Grumps, let's talk about this famous hat of yours. How does it fit into your story? We seem to have stalled."

"Patience lad, patience, I'm getting there.

"So, we visited the falls and had a great time with a guide that knew the best places for photography. The waterfalls fairly take your breath away, and the noise! all that water tumbling and crashing, I've got some photos I'll show you later." I said.

"Sounds amazing, a trip of a lifetime, I imagine."

"It was lad, but that's not even the half of it, because then we went on to the Chobe National

Park for what turned out to be ten days of sheer joy and excitement."

"Staying in traditional wooden cabins, we were right in amongst the wild animals, where you could sit on the porch and hear such a variety of creatures, Lions, Coyotes, Wildebeest, and the Cicadas were deafening.

Then, after a couple of days, an invitation came to visit an elephant sanctuary, a refuge for orphaned or abused animals. We got to work with the wardens, feeding and caring for the elephants. Some were sick, and others just needed company, and there was always plenty to do for us tourists."

"No way!" I shrieked, "getting so close to all those different animals, I did not know that you were both so adventurous. I suppose that was when you needed the hat?"

"No, the hat came later. I told you, be patient. There was a large female elephant called Maggie that came into the compound every day for food and water. She had an infant but kept it outside in the bush, I suppose, for protection. She was so sweet and would lift a warden with her trunk and place him ever so gently on her back, or she'd roll over while we hosed her down to keep her cool.

We became good friends, and she would trust us, we had confidence in her not to hurt us.

"We, your gran, and I had our own room, with mesh over the windows to keep out mosquitos. We felt fairly safe, but I never expected something bigger to get into the room, but it did."

"A lion?" I asked excitedly, not ready for his answer.

"Nope, I felt a tugging at the bedclothes down by my feet, but it was so dark I could not see a thing, although I could hear something breathing, something big, so I reached out for my flashlight and got the shock of my life, because there was Maggie, our friendly elephant, at the window with her trunk pushed through the mesh trying to attract my attention."

"Weren't you frightened?" I had to ask, trying to imagine this huge animal forcing its trunk through the window.

"What about gran, she must have scared out of her wits?" I suggested.

"No, not a bit."

"I was more surprised than anything, and your gran slept through the whole thing. Grabbing my clothes, I went outside to work out what was happening. When she saw me, Maggie our friendly elephant.

"She lifted her trunk and tried to wrap it around my shoulders, pulling me to where she was heading. When she walked away, I knew she wanted me to follow. Something was wrong. So, I followed as best I could, tripping on branches and bushes until we finally got to a clearing, and there it was."

"Where what was Grumps? What did you find there?" I asked, fearing the worst.

"I came across the little one. She had one leg trapped in the fork of a dead tree and was exhausted from trying to free herself."

"What did you do? What *could* you do, Grumps?" I asked him.

"What do you think I did, lad? I saved it, of course. I eased it's leg out gently even though the baby was thrashing around wildly, but it was too weak to stand. Then the mother attended to the youngster while I watched and then she looked at me.

The moon was giving a bit of light and I could see the emotion in her eyes, and a 'knowing' look of gratitude that made me feel very humble and small. I then crept back to the hut and got back into bed."

"We left the camp the following day and nobody else knew or heard anything about it. You're the only person I've ever told."

I was speechless for a moment, then asked, "What about that wretched hat? How does that fit into this story?"

"Oh, the hat, yes, I forgot about that bit. I bought it in the souvenir shop at the airport as we were leaving."

5.
Grumps the furniture mover

Arriving at my grandparent's house one Saturday morning I was surprised to find them 'curtain twitching,' you know, peering out through a window at the neighbours and trying not to be seen. The silence that met me as I walked in was absolute, and now standing there behind them I was afraid to speak for fear of making them jump out of their skins.

But my grandfather knew I was there and turning, he beckoned me to come over, he never said a word; he just put his fingers to his lips as if to say 'shush.'

"What on earth are you doing" I whispered sliding in to join them by the window.

"We're having some fun watching this caper, come and join in the fun" he suggested.

Grumps spoke quietly trying not to laugh, then pointing to a young couple across the road who were trying to load up a removal van he said.

"What do you make of that for a lark?" nudging me in the chest with his elbow. I pulled up a chair and sat next to them to see what all the fuss was about. It was not long before a young couple came out of the house carrying an exceptionally large mattress.

It kept folding in the middle as they struggled to walk with it, and then trying to get it in the van was hilarious to see as it had a mind of its own, bending and buckling until they threw it down in frustration. We could not hear what they were saying to each other, but their faces were a picture and told a story without words. This went on for another ten minutes before the novelty wore off and we regained our composure and moved away back into the room.

Grumps was the first to speak,

"What do you think gran?" He said turning to my grandmother, how about we get the lad some tea and the posh biscuits, to make him feel welcome?" Gran spoke up,

"When you say 'we' I take that to mean me? Well at least we'll get a decent cuppa," she half-joked. Then very obligingly Gran shuffled off to make the tea, this, she *was* extremely good at.

She had decreed sometime in the murky past that he, Grumps, should not be allowed to make any more tea, since he was so bad at it. Gran stopped at the kitchen door, turned around and spoke mockingly.

"If you want to tell him a story, why don't you tell him about your tea-making skills, eh? Tell him how you boiled the eggs for breakfast and then used the hot water to make a pot of tea, tell him that if you dare."

"Now don't take too much notice of Gran, she still doesn't understand how home economics work," Grumps whispered as she shuffled away, although he waited until she was out of hearing range. This sort of sparring with words was quite normal and they seemed to thrive on it, both giving as good as each other.

"Home economics? How do you mean Grumps?" I enjoyed listening to his theories, always thinking that I might learn something, which I did sometimes, but not always.

Grumps looked at me with a mischievous smile, this he would do when Gran had cornered him.

"Well, it goes back to after the war, when there was a shortage of food and services like water, coal and electricity we had to economise, and a pan of precious boiling water could serve more than one purpose. So, when the boiled eggs were done, I made a pot of tea with the water, rather than throwing it away, you see? That is what I call home economics, simple, don't you agree?"

It did sound logical to my young mind, but I couldn't resist asking him.

"What did it taste like? It must have been a bit rough, I mean, just thinking where an egg has been."

Grumps replied,

"It was deeelicious." He stretched out the word while putting on a pained expression.

I fell about laughing and nearly knocked the tea tray flying as Gran was placing it on the table, she had a different take on his story and couldn't help butting in with,

"It was disgusting! Don't tell the lad lies, it tasted like dishwater, and you know it, you were just too lazy to do the job properly, home economics? Born lazy, that's more like the truth" and picking up a tea towel she flicked him lightly on his back with one end and went off to get the biscuits.

We had our tea and biscuits without further incident, except that with every sip of tea Grumps would say, "Deeeelicious" and Gran would flick him with tea towel Grumps got up from the table and saying,

"Well, never mind all that now, there's a bit of early morning fun and games across the road, such larks I've not seen since…well it was when I had to move some furniture some years ago. Did I ever tell you that story lad, about moving furniture in the rain and mud with brother Mike? It was like a burglary in reverse."

I tried to recall the story, but I couldn't.

"No Grumps, I don't remember that one, did you have fun and games like that couple over there?"

"Oh, it was worse than that, me lad, no it was like something out of a madcap comedy movie, although at the time it wasn't funny, and it could have got us into a lot of trouble, it's probably ok to laugh about it now after all these years."

"Really? Tell me Grumps" I was getting interested by this time,

"And why was it so dodgy?" Grumps saw my expression, and he was going to take full advantage; I was going to get the entire story, another good one, perhaps?

Gran went over to her sewing table saying,

"I'll leave you two to talk, although I doubt if the youngster will do much talking, he'll get an ear-bashing as usual." I was sixteen but my Gran still called me a 'youngster.'

"C'mon lad," Grumps took my arm and ushered me over to the comfy chairs; he grabbed some more of the 'posh' biscuits, 'just in case' he whispered, and we sat down.

I was never quite sure what the 'just in case' meant but I suspect it had something to do with Gran clearing them away too quickly and him feeling cheated or short-changed in the biscuit department.

"Now where was I, oh yes the true story of the burglary in reverse." He mumbled with a mouth full of biscuit.

"Your Gran will swear to the truth of this story,

because she was there," I looked back at my grandmother, and she nodded and smiled giving her approval.

Grumps finally got started.

"I used to live in an enormous house at the edge of town, a dark foreboding place that was much too big for me. I had a look around for a smaller place and finally settled on an old, converted farmhouse.

It was a lot smaller, and I realised I had too much stuff to take with me. Now, the furniture I had was too good to throw away, and the question was, what to do with it? After a bit of head-scratching, I asked around to see if any of my friends could store it somewhere. And after a couple of days of asking someone suggested that I talk to an old friend Dee, who lived at the other end of town.

She came up with a plan; I could store as much as I wanted in her large house if I followed her instructions to the letter. She told me that there were empty rooms in her house but that her husband must not find out I had put stuff in there."

Intrigued, I asked Grumps,

"How on earth would someone not know if their house was being used as storage, it doesn't make sense, does it?

"You're quite right lad, it didn't make sense, till she told me that her husband would come home from work, walk in through the front door, into his office, and after that, he would go to bed, get up the next day, walk out in the morning and repeat the whole thing day after day.

There were rooms that he never went into according to Dee, and if I could get the stuff into a couple of those rooms, then I would be high and dry. Dee explained that they would be out the following evening and I had a couple of hours to get it done.

She would ring when they were going out and I was to take the furniture round during the time they were absent. Dee would arrange for the housekeeper to be ready for us, and to let us in. It sounded ok but a bit tight."

I interrupted again with.

"A bit tight? Sounds downright impossible to me, surely the husband wouldn't be that dumb, would he? You're not stringing me along here are you Grumps?"

I gave a glance at my grandmother for verification, and she nodded, saying,

"Yes, so far, it's all true."

Grumps had taken advantage of this interruption by grabbing another biscuit, so, with a mouth half stuffed he went on.

"I called up my brother Mike, told him to come around with a horsebox, and we filled it to the top as best we could, it took us a few hours, then we locked it up overnight.

We waited around the next evening for the phone call, six o'clock came, and we waited, we started to get nervous and twitchy, ten minutes to seven more twitchy and then at seven it rang and made us jump, even though we had been waiting for it, our nerves were on edge."

"So, they had left the house, and we were to set off on this mad brain scheme. And then it started raining, it got harder, and the sky got darker, it had been fairly light earlier which would have given us a better chance, but now it was disastrous."

"What did you do?" I asked.

"We carried out the plan and towed the horse box with all the furniture around to the big house, drove around to the back as directed, which meant driving over the grass, parked up and banged on the back French doors."

"The housekeeper looked with disbelief at two soaking wet men with a horse box parked on the precious grass and a lot of furniture to unload, but she pointed to the staircase and told us which rooms to go to, then she disappeared inside."

Grumps stopped the story for a moment to catch his breath as he was getting agitated as if he were there again on that fateful evening. After a few seconds, he continued.

"We had these great lumping bits of wardrobes, tables, chairs, all sorts to carry up the stairs, that had a cream-coloured carpet as did the landing and hallway, cream mind you! and us with our muddy boots, knocking pictures off the walls as we went up, chipping paint off here and there, and all the time we knew that they could come back at any time."

"We finally got it all in, just in time as the housekeeper received the call saying that the owners were about to leave the restaurant and were coming home. They would be about half an hour and if they had caught us there our goose would have been cooked."

"Goose?" I asked. "What's this about a goose"?

"Haven't you heard that expression,

"My goose is cooked"? It means the game is up, I've been found out. Anyway, we got into the car, started it up and tried to drive off, but no chance."

"Why not, what happened?" I could feel myself getting tense at this point, would they get caught? It all sounded very exciting and dangerous.
Grumps went on.

"We couldn't believe it, the wheels had no traction on the wet grass and to make it worse, the wheels were sinking into the ground, the more we revved the engine the deeper we went, we were stuffed.

The housekeeper came out shrieking about how we were all 'done for.' Then I saw a couple of coconut door mats and grabbed them from inside the house, stuffed them under the wheels and with one last almighty effort we got onto the harder ground and away. Driving out we passed the owners on their way home, and of course, they knew nothing about us, or at least, the husband didn't. We left the poor housekeeper wondering what had happened to her quiet evening."

"Well Grumps, come on, how did that go down with the husband when he found out and did the housekeeper get into any trouble?

"We waited and watched for days, to see if there was any sign of him finding out and after a couple of weeks I bumped into Dee in the street and asked her if there was any "fall-out" from that evening."

"Oh no," she told me,

"He hasn't said a word, I told you that he doesn't use those rooms and he never goes round to the back of the house, and the mess was sorted out by our housekeeper, so it's all good."

Turning to my Grandmother I asked, "What did Grumps mean when he said that you were there, what part did you play in all that confusion."

My Grandmother looked up from her sewing and said smiling,

"Who do you think the housekeeper was that night?

Your Grandfather visited me secretly when the owners of the house were out, I would phone to let him know the coast was clear and so the relationship blossomed, we found it difficult to keep up the secrecy, so he asked me to marry him and move into his cottage.

And you know? He still can't make a decent cup of tea, and I've never really forgiven him for the mess he made moving the furniture, I had a lot of trouble cleaning it up."

Grumps gave a wry smile, looked very 'sheepish' and grabbed another biscuit before they were snatched them away from him.

6.
That was our time.

Warning: Contains historical discriminative language.

Along the embankment, beside the River Thames in the City of London, there are many benches. They are curious in their design, in so far as the sides or ends of these benches are shaped like camels sitting on the ground. Complete with saddle packs, they form part of the bench, with the end of each seat resting on a camel's back.

They might not seem important to you or me, but to a lot of homeless people, these benches provide a bed for the night, with either cardboard or old bits of carpet as blankets.

I had just returned from a college trip to London where seeing this came as a shock to me as we live in a very quiet village, and I had never seen anything like it for real, only in TV broadcasts. It made such an impression, so much so, that on the following Saturday I went to discuss it with Grumps, my grandfather. When I arrived, I found him in his den, as was usual on the weekends. It was cold and damp outside, but the little potbellied stove kept it as warm as toast on the inside.

"Ah, young un, not much of a day, is it?" he said

when I walked in.

"I'm surprised to see you today, what with all this wet weather."

I told him it would take more than a bit of dampness to keep me away.

"I shoulda known it, it's not often that you stay away on a Saturday, pull y'self up a chair by the stove, and come and dry y'self, then you can tell me about that college trip to London."

He had warm, homemade mulled wine sitting on the stove, and the sweet fragrance of the spices filled the air, and that, mixed with the aromatic tobacco that he smoked in his pipe, was just delightful, and a warm glow came over me.

"What was that you were listening to on the radio when I came in? I heard someone mention ghosts, you're not going all 'Spooky' on me, are you Grumps?" I joked, moving a little closer to the fire.

"No, it was a bunch of scientists and religious folks discussing the 'afterlife,' as if we haven't got enough to worry about with this life, eh lad?"

"You're right there Grumps. Only last week I saw some miserable scenes on the Embankment in London when I went on the college trip. I wanted to talk to you about it if you've got the time?"

Then I told Grumps what I'd seen and how upsetting it had been.

Grumps said,

"Yes, it can come as a bit of a shock, especially if you've lived a life away from the city as we do. But those situations are not new. It's been happening in one form or another for generations. The poor, living in the shadow of the wealthy, those with nothing, being passed over by the well to do.

It's a bit of a coincidence, you saw that along the embankment, 'cos I used to live in London, many years ago, and I would often walk along there and see people in that situation, men and women, mostly ex-service folks.

In the years after the war, personnel that had outlived their usefulness were dismissed to make their way in the world by themselves, where employment was scarce. We used to call it 'paddle your own canoe'

"That sounds terrible," I said, "even after serving their country?"

"Sadly, yes." He answered.

Grumps thought for a moment, then pulled out an old, crumpled photo from a shoe box, his 'filing system' he jokingly called it. He handed me the photo of a Jamaican airman in a British Air Force uniform, then said.

"I met this man on one of my walks along the embankment. His name was Bill, and he told me a story, a very interesting one, I think. Do you want to hear about this man? There may be ghosts involved."

"Ghosts? I queried, 'Really? In this day and age? With all we know about science and physics, that would be a bit far-fetched to me."

"Well, you make your mind up after you've heard it. Deal?" Grumps asked.

Trying not to laugh, I said.

"Go on then" 'I'll humour him.' I thought to myself.

Grumps pulled out his tobacco pouch, re-filled his pipe, poured out a couple of glasses of the warm spiced wine, and sat down to tell me his tale.

"As I was saying, on one of my walks by the River Thames, I saw this chap on one of those benches, he had an old cap on the pavement that had a few coins in it, and I added a few of my own, it was a chill evening, and that way he might buy a hot drink from one of the vendors dotted about the place."

"He looked up briefly to acknowledge the coins. I asked him his name, and he told me it was Bill. So, I sat down beside him to chat. He seemed grateful for the company, and after a while, I asked him about his circumstances, and how he came to be there. This was Bill's story:"

"One Autumn evening, as the nights were getting colder, Bill was sitting on one of those benches looking into the misty Thames in front of him, not thinking about anything, when he noticed someone sitting beside him.'

"He had not seen him arrive, but turning toward the stranger, Bill glanced at his profile, and then he felt a shiver, thinking that he'd recognised him, but his young age ruled that out, and so he thought no more about it."

After a minute or two, the young man spoke to Bill, asking."

'Hey ol' fella, what's the story with the coat? I've seen you up here every day. You always wear it come rain or shine, day or night. There must be a story there?'

"Bill looked around to the young guy who was in his early twenties next to him, he was smartly dressed and sounded genuinely interested, not one of the usual layabouts you'd see around there at night, there was something about him that Bill could not place, but he did warm to him, so he replied.

"A story, eh? Yep, there's a story. How long have you got?" Bill asked him. The young man shrugged his shoulders and spoke quietly.

'Dunno, as long as it takes, I suppose.'

"So, there on a cold November evening, the ex-serviceman told his story to someone who seemed willing to listen, turning to the youngster.

Bill told him."

"I love this old coat, people stare I know, sometimes they point and mock, but I still love it, you can almost hear them saying

'Why's that old black man wearing a Military coat?' so, before I start, let me ask you a question, do know where Jamaica is?"

The young guy seemed surprised by that but replied,

'Yes, of course, it's in the Caribbean. Why?'

"Well," Bill continued, "here's the funny or sad part; I came to England in Nineteen Forty from Jamaica, I had saved some money, and with the help of my Father I bought a ticket on a steamer, I came to help with the war effort, and having had some experience in engineering I thought it would go well for me.

On arrival, I turned up at the Air Force recruitment office to join up. Some senior chap asked me where I had come from, I told them 'Kingston', and on hearing this an officer suggested I go to my local office to sign up, I told him. "Kingston Jamaica, not Kingston-on-Thames"

The senior officer looked confused and spoke up. 'Never heard of it' but a recruit jumped in with,

'Sir, I think I know where Jamaica is. It's in West Africa, pretty sure of that, sir,'

I thought to myself, "Here we go, ignorant sod, not a good start, but things were to get worse."

"It started with Monkey jokes and unfriendly remarks, then, when it came to going out together, the local girls were off-limits, so it was very unpleasant for me as you can imagine."

"I won't bore you with stories of 'heroic' air battles, and Air Force life, no, it was the life away from the camp, and then after the war was over, that was very hard for me."

Bill looked around at my attentive companion. He was still listening, but in total silence, you could say transfixed.

"Anyway," Bill continued,

"When I went on leave for the weekend it was always, 'No Vacancies' at the guest houses, some even had signs in the windows saying, 'No Irish, No Blacks, No Dogs,' can you imagine being put in the same group as dogs?"

On hearing that part, Bill's companion stood up.

'No way!' He shouted, 'Are you having me on?' Bill had to tell him that sadly that it was true, even having fought for this country, that was how he had been treated."

"So, anyway, about the coat, by the way, have you got a spare cigarette please?" Bill asked his new companion. He handed Bill a cigarette, and Bill continued.

"I had one close friend, a Polish airman named Joe who had experienced similar prejudice, even though he was white, he was still a foreigner, he looked out for me, and even found me somewhere to stay after the war, finding work for us both, which lasted a while until we were put out on the streets, when the company closed, as business was bad."

"So now we were 'Gentlemen of the Road,' that's what they called people like us in those days. Bill explained, we begged and scrounged food where we could. We would walk and talk and make these benches our beds for the night; this was

'Home,' and Joe had a saying, 'This is our time, Bill, our time. We must make the most of it, because we don't get another shot at it.'

"Then, one winter, a few years back," Bill went on to say, we went looking for shelter. It was a bitter evening with the temperature dropping fast, and we needed to take care. Joe suggested a bombed-out building that had never been rebuilt after the war, and we had to keep warm to survive. The walls were ready to collapse and so picking our way across the old timbers was dangerous. Beams would crack under our weight and the stench of dead rats, and the dust was overpowering.

"We found the driest spot, cleared a space as best we could, then settled down for the night. Joe was stronger than me and took his coat off and put it over me to protect me from the frost."

"When I awoke, Joe was dead beside me, frozen stiff, and it is because of his kindness, that I swore I would wear this coat, his coat, that had saved my life, until the end of my days. I still fancy he is there with me, and I talk to him sometimes when I get depressed. But I carried on living on the street on my own.

He is always there with me, in spirit, at least. I fancy I hear him, or catch a glimpse of him sometimes, but it is only the mist and shadows, a trick of the light, maybe?"

Grumps said, "Bill told me he must have fallen asleep, and when he awoke, his new buddy had gone. Although he hadn't blamed him, it had been a miserable evening."

"It was a couple of weeks before Bill saw him again. Then one misty, murky evening, he rocked up, smiling and grinning like a Cheshire cat. The stranger held out an envelope and nodded."

'Open it, go on, it's for you.'

"Bill was confused and asked, "What's this all about young 'un?" Bill opened it to find a twenty-pound note,

'It's yours,' he said. 'I wrote your story for a writing competition for college and won, so it's only fair, it's yours.'

"He turned and walked away. Bill found that he

could not speak with shock, he tried shouting after him."

"What's your name kid?" the stranger stopped, looked back.

'My name's also Joe.' "He whispered as he slipped away into the mist, then Bill could hear him muttering, something about the time, 'that *really* was *our* time.' very faintly, then he was gone, this was no trick of the light, surely?"

Grumps said,

"I had to leave Bill at that point, to get back home, as it was getting late, but just as I was getting ready to go, I turned around and watched him stretch out on the bench, then he passed away, peacefully, with a smile, right next to me."

Grumps stopped talking and showed me a grubby piece of paper, a £20 note, saying,

"Bill gave me this, just before he died, the banknote he had kept as a memento, also this photo of himself, and so I thought you might like to hear his story, to see what you make of it all."

I stood up, I had a lump in my throat, touched Grumps on the shoulder, smiled, and then left quietly, without saying a word.

7.
The Dancing Lady

My grandpa Grumps was very dark-skinned. This was due to two things; the time he spent abroad in hot countries, and when at home he was always gardening. He was an outdoor man.

I also think that the only time he was happy indoors was when he was in his shed, or den, as he preferred to call it. There he could do what he wanted, drink whatever he liked, sleep or work on his model making. It was his 'Kingdom' and my grandmother rarely went in there, except to wake him up for supper sometimes.

He was prone to falling asleep after drinking his home-made beer or wine, and this was where he would make and drink it. It was also the only place that my grandmother allowed him to smoke his pipe.

Grumps had many that he'd collected from all over the world, allegedly when on his travels. There was a rack in the den with about thirty different pipes; some were hand-carved and decorated in wonderful shapes and designs.

My favourite was in the shape of a buffalo's head where the carving was exquisite. You could see the hair and whiskers and even the eyes were realistic, appearing to follow you around the room when

Grumps moved his head. I also had a favourite tobacco that I liked him to smoke whenever I went there. It had an aroma that was difficult to identify, but I thought I could detect chestnut and apple.

One very hot August day, I went to see Grumps and found him in his den. He'd already started on a bottle of brew and was dozing off in the heat of the day.

On his right upper arm, Grumps had a faded tattoo, an image of a scantily clad woman, which must have been very colourful when it was first done, and when I was younger, he would flex his muscles and make the woman 'dance' to amuse me. However, my grandmother did not find it amusing and would scold him for being rude and improper. In his later years, he would keep it covered up, and I had the impression that it slightly embarrassed him. I had forgotten all about the tattoo, as I hadn't seen it for a long time.

On that day he had removed his long-sleeved shirt because of the heat, revealing the tattoo, and I took the opportunity to ask him.

"Grumps, where did you get the tattoo? Is there a story behind it? I remember you used to make it dance when I was younger, and that always made me laugh."

"Ah, the naughty tattoo, the dancing lady, yes that

kept you amused. It's very faded now due to me spending so much time in the sun, gardening and travelling."

"You know me well enough to know there's a story there somewhere, and there is, me boyo, although it's not one that I'm very proud of, perhaps I'll tell you when you're older."

"I knew it, c'mon Grumps, I'm not a child, and you'd be surprised at some of the things I hear at college. Have you got the time to talk about it now?" I asked him, expecting him to tell me to come back later 'cos he was busy, but he thought about it for a minute and then decided he was happy to stop what he was doing as it was getting hotter, and he didn't feel very energetic. He also liked an excuse to open another bottle of his home-made beer or wine, and this time was no different.

"I've got cold beer in the cool box. Fetch some more over and I'll tell you about this tattoo. You'll probably think I'm very foolish by the end, but you can decide for yourself."

I brought over a couple of bottles, poured out for us both, then sat back in one of the dusty, old leather armchairs. This sent a cloud of dust into the air making me cough, which prompted Grumps to say,

"There, you see, it's a dusty old job and the only

cure is a little 'light' refreshment."

I couldn't help but laugh at the way he would always justify having a drink, there would always be a good reason. After a few moments, he asked, a little confused.

"What was I going to talk about? Oh yes, the tattoo, funny business really, and such a long time ago, you can hardly see it now. It's faded so much, but at the time it was so colourful."

He stopped speaking again and seemed to lose the thread. He was now into his nineties, and this was quite normal, so I prompted him.

"The tattoo Grumps, where and how did you get it? Remember? You were telling me."

"Oh yes, that bloomin' tattoo."

"It was not long after I'd finished my apprenticeship. I had little money, so I went on a merchant ship for a couple of voyages to boost my income. This was before I met and married your gran. I kept the tattoo hidden from her while we were courting, you know, going out together. But of course, she found out on our wedding night, if you get my meaning?" He said with a wink.

It took me a few seconds before I got his 'meaning', but he had already moved on with his story.

"Anyway." he continued.

"We tied up in Shanghai after being on the ocean for weeks, and I went with some of the lads ashore for a quiet drink."

Grumps stopped and flexed his muscle, making the tattoo appear to dance.

"A quiet drink I tells ya." Grumps said doing a Popeye impression, and then he laughed hysterically and nearly choked on his beer. It was a couple of minutes before he was ready to carry on.

"So, while we were drinking and minding our own business, some local girls came and sat with us, and when we moved on, they followed us, and the same thing happened the next place we went to. They followed us everywhere we went, getting really pesky, you know, annoying us."

"Couldn't you shake them off? What did they want?" I asked naively.

"I suppose they wanted a bit of fun, free drinks and possibly a British husband. I must say that they were bewitching with their youthful looks and flattering words."

"Sounds like they were a right pain." I said with youthful ignorance.

"Oh, they were, they were me lad." Grumps said, looking around nervously to see if my gran was listening.

"We found out that they were 'showgirls,' you know, dancers and all that, but they got fed up with us when we stopped buying them drinks and they cleared off into the night. Then my group of mates started singing sea-shanties in the alleyways and the police chased us off. That's when we got split up and I went off to find somewhere to sleep.

After looking into a couple of boarding houses, I found one that was not as dirty as the others, but it turned out that the house was being used by the girls who had been with us earlier. There was a right old party going on downstairs and as I couldn't sleep, I went and joined them. This went on all night until I fell asleep in a corner."

"When I awoke, I walked about a bit, and then saw my mates in a tattoo shop. Still a bit boozy I went in, sat down and I fell asleep again, and when I opened my eyes the next time, the tattoo artist wanted money from me. When I asked why, he told me.

'You came in shouting, Dancing lady! dancing lady! I want a dancing lady! So, I gave you the tattoo of a dancing lady you asked for.'

Of course, my gran' had been listening, she'd been standing outside all along, keeping very quiet. Although I suspect she already knew the story, and that was the first time I saw Grumps blush, despite having dark skin.

8.
The Road Trip

My grandfather Grumps loved his old car, and even into his long retirement he had always washed and polished it himself.
But during his last years he'd taken to sharing that experience with me, he said that it would be good practice for me after I told him that I was going to try to earn some money from car washing in our village.

So, he offered me an unpaid job looking after his beloved black 1937 Humber, he knew of course that I would never have asked for any money, it also drew us closer together with him treating me more like an adult and an equal.

Eventually of course he had to give up driving, but he would not part with the car, telling me,

"When I'm gone, you can do what you like with it, use it as my coffin, it won't trouble me none, it might even be worth a few quid, but till then it stays here with me."

Well, that was clear enough, and he meant it, in fact, he never wasted words and always meant what he said and said what he meant. So, after he passed on it went to a collector who would cherish it and show it off at car rallies.

Holiday times were great with Grumps, as he would take us away for a couple of weeks each summer in his prized Humber, and there was always a bit of ceremony involved.

He would tell us at what time exactly to be ready, then he would turn into our road majestically, slowly rolling up to our gate so that all the neighbours could watch and admire.

I looked forward to these times and would go to the gate and watch for him coming, only to run back inside shouting with glee,

"He's here, he's here, Grumps is outside, c'mon let's go." Then I would pull my overloaded suitcase along the floor and the path, scraping the leather all the way.

On opening the car doors, I could smell the old leather seats and the furniture polish that he used to shine up the walnut dashboard and steering wheel. The wood trim made it look 'Regal' and when I sat on the back seats I felt like Royalty. The other distinctive smells were the warm oil, and the chrome and paint polish around the bonnet area, where the engine had started to get hot.

I re-live those days when I talk about my grandfather; he *was* a grandfather like no other.

And then there was the motorcycle, another one of his treasures, a Triumph TR5 Trophy built in the late Fifties. It was still in showroom condition, even after being laid up under covers for years.

He would unwrap it from time to time and keep it polished and spotless, even though he had stopped riding it years ago.

Grumps had never talked much about his motorcycling days until one day I cornered him in his garage, just as he was unwrapping the Triumph.

"Hey Grumps," I said, startling him,

"What you up to now, thinking about taking to the road again?" I said teasing him.

"You can mock, but I've ridden halfway around the world and back when I was younger of course. I expect your parents have told you, eh?"

"I know that you were a bit of a tearaway, winding up the local police with your mates back in the day," I said giving him a gentle nudge in the ribs. Grumps explained,

"We used to play tricks on the local police, like speeding and then hiding the bikes."

“How did that work Grumps,” I asked, “tell me some more, that sounds like fun.”
“Well, we all used to meet up, all my biker mates, in a Café called the El Cabana on the A2. After a while we would get a bit bored, same old music on the jukebox, same conversations, so we devised a little competition between ourselves, and it went like this.”

“We would take turns to get on our bikes and wait on the main road, as soon as a police car went by, we would open the throttle, overtake and try to reach 100 miles an hour by the time we reached the first roundabout, then we’d go around and come straight back and hide the bike around the back of the café. The cops would come to where we were, ‘cos they knew we were a bit of a handful and ask to see the rider off such and such number plate.”

“The rider would then tell the officer that someone had nicked his bike while he was drinking his coffee and that he’d been there all the time minding his own business, when in fact he was guilty, and the bike was hidden. To us, it was harmless fun at the time, and I would not condone behaviour like that.”

Grumps said, giving me a stern look in case I had any ideas of copying him.

"Don't worry Grumps, I would not dream of doing such a thing," I assured him with my fingers crossed behind my back and suggested that we give his bike a bit of a polish and cover it up again, and half an hour later we had finished, and it looked like a new bike.

Grumps wanted to lock up the garage and go back down to his Den, where he thought we might be more comfortable. I agreed, knowing that he meant he wanted a drink, and a smoke of his pipe, and that was fine with me as I could feel another story coming on, and I was not wrong.

Once we were back in his Den we settled into the old leather armchairs, so now with pipe fully loaded and drinks dispensed, he wanted to tell me about an incident when he nearly didn't make it, when he was given a ride on the back of his friends Triumph Bonneville.

"May the good Lord strike me down if I tell a lie, but I came within inches from death, and it happened like this. When I started my apprenticeship, I made friends with a keen biker like m'self, we were passionate about our bikes and talked of very little else."

"I was buying a second-hand Honda 250 cc, a one hundred miles an hour model, but was waiting for the shop to service it before I took delivery. Now, my mate, Peter told me not to worry because he would give me a lift home on his Triumph."

"We were working alongside each other so that seemed like the answer, however, during that day,

Peter had done something silly by jumping up to swing on an overhead pipe, but what he didn't know was that the pipe carried boiling water from the laundry and so he burnt his hands quite badly. After a spell in the First-Aid room, he came out all bandaged up, both hands!"

"So now where did that leave us? as he would be giving me a lift back home, but with both hands out of action I couldn't see it happening. But I was wrong, 'cos he had decided to ride his bike anyway, with both hands in such a state."

"Oh no!" I gasped, "weren't you worried? that sounds reckless, just plain stupid."

"Strangely enough I wasn't overly concerned because I knew he was a brilliant rider and believed that he wouldn't have attempted it if he wasn't confident, so I trusted him."

"When we started out, he was a bit shaky, but within a few seconds he had control of the bike and we set off."

"The road was just wide enough for buses to pass each other, and they were constantly on the move in both directions, so we set off up the hill".

"Now, Pete was not one for riding behind another vehicle, that was too slow for him, so he decided to overtake the bus in front, but he miscalculated the speed of the bus coming towards us, which was bearing down on us, face on".

"That oncoming bus would arrive while we were overtaking the other one, so, he shouted, *"HOLD ON!"* which I did of course, and we just about passed between them."

"My two shoulders rubbed against both buses, but he had kept his nerve and stayed focused on the gap, and him being slimmer than me had not felt a thing, but he was shocked and apologetic for me being so scared."

"I was very happy to take delivery of my bike soon after, where I could control my destiny because that had been a very 'close shave.' "

"Did you behave yourself on your bike, after that scare?" I asked.

"I must have done; I am still here ain't I?" he laughed.

I suggested,

"Perhaps you found it safer to drive the car, at least you can't fall off."

Grumps laughed and said,

"Maybe, but I still managed to have some fun and games in cars." He said lighting his pipe again,

"Fetch some more drinks and I'll tell you about a remarkable journey that I made with some friends in a Vauxhall Cresta."

So, drinks were fetched, and I sat back to hear more of his tales. Grumps started.

"Me and two friends used to go down to Cornwall at the weekends, we would set off about ten P.M. and drive through the night reaching Lands' End around six o'clock in the morning.

I had a provisional licence at that time, but I could drive accompanied as the others held full licences.

The car of choice was a Vauxhall Cresta owned by Peter one of the friends.

A big roomy car that had an American look about it, very comfy. We had made this journey quite a few times without incident, it was three hundred and fifty miles each way.

We set off from Kent where we lived and travelled across the country, and on one part of the journey we had to drive across Salisbury Plain."

I interrupted with,

"Salisbury Plain, that's where the Army do their training isn't it?"

Grumps smiled and said,

"Yes, and that's where the problem was, with us, we were on the plain with tanks rolling over the hills and we broke down." I gave Grumps a look as if to say,

"Oh, you *really* landed yourselves in it."

"Yep." he replied."

"We were on the way back and it was a dark and gloomy afternoon, night was approaching, and we were aware that the Army was there on manoeuvres, firing rockets, bazookas, hand grenades and I don't dare to think what else."

"Tanks?" I suggested.

"Yes, tanks as well, we couldn't see them, but we could hear them. But we were not so sure that they'd seen us, as there were bangs and explosions right close to us.

There was a pub we had passed half a mile back, so we walked to find assistance, no luck there as it was closed.

Then someone stopped to check if we were in trouble, so Peter showed him the
gearstick. He held it up and said, "Yes, look, the gearstick has come out of its socket."

"Oh crikey!" the stranger exclaimed, "that's not good, no, no, it's not good at all."

Coming closer to have a look, he said,

"I can't fix it, but I can tell you what's happened, and how you might be able to drive it away from here."

We looked at each other in disbelief, but we were ready to listen. The stranger came over and said,

"This model has a linkage to the gearbox, it's not connected straight into it, and if you're lucky you can use a large screwdriver to move the front part, this will in turn move the part that *is* connected." He said, "let me show you."

He came over, took a large screwdriver out of our toolbox, placed it in the link and demonstrated, "It involves one person steering, one to use this screwdriver and one to keep a lookout so that you don't hit anything because you will need your wits about you."

Grumps put on his serious voice and said,

"We looked at each other again, with even more disbelief as the prospect looked grim.

However, we had no choice, that or risk being target practice, we were tired teenagers, and it did not take much to scare us."

I interrupted Grumps again with,

"How far did you have to drive back home, using this method?"

"Oh, it was about a three-hour drive, over one hundred miles I suppose, anyway we were determined, and we did it like this."

"Pete would operate the screwdriver, my other mate Nobby would steer and push down on the clutch as Pete changed gear, and I was to 'lookout,' shouting directions.

"We started it up and made our first tentative attempts to drive like that, luckily, we were out in the sticks with very little traffic around to start with.

"So, off we went with Nobby shouting,

'Clutch in' to Pete who obliged by moving the screwdriver, 'second gear!' Nobby barked, and Pete moved the linkage again, and all the while I was watching out for cars coming from all directions."

"Nothing coming," I would say each time, even if there was, I just wanted to get home as quickly as possible."

"We drove like this for what seemed a lifetime, roundabouts were relatively easy as we could judge the speed and approach of the other traffic and it didn't slow us down much."

"Junctions were more difficult if we had to stop, and traffic lights of course, luckily in those days there were few. So, it went on, 'Second!' 'Clutch!' 'Gear change!' 'All clear!' or 'something coming,' 'slow down!' and it was starting to get dark, to make things worse, although I suppose it was good that nobody could see the three 'mad teenagers' shouting and driving one car.'

I now looked at Grumps with new admiration, and greater respect, as I imagined the three of them hooting and hollering whilst driving on the A 303, trying not to get shot at, I just had to laugh, what a picture?

9.

Food For Thought

The idea of burying people lying down has always seemed a bit of a strange idea to me. What if they buried people upright? Wouldn't they take up less space and you could get more bodies in a graveyard?

It was thoughts like this that often ran through my mind as a teenager. I was curious about the world, but at school, there was this notion that a child needed to know facts and figures and not much else.

Luckily my grandfather, Grumps, who knew everything, remember? He would know all about these things. He had been places, done a lot in his life, and I trusted him. It was also true that he told stories, some of which were far-fetched, but Grumps was someone that I could turn to for answers and advice concerning serious matters.

I was closer to him than to my father, who was rarely home. This was because of his work as a Merchant Seaman and Dad would be away for months at a time.

One day, on our way back from watching a football match, the opportunity came to ask him about my burial question. As we passed the cemetery, I stopped to look over the wall, and I talked about it with Grumps. He paused, thought about it for a moment, then said.

"Not only do they bury people lying down, but they also bury 'em face downwards, do you know why?" He said with his most serious face on.

"No, honestly? But why?" I asked, feeling shocked.

"It's to stop the buggers pushing the lids open to escape." He said, roaring with laughter,

"If folks have a made a mistake and they are not quite dead, imagine that." It sounded quite horrible, but now I knew he was teasing when he burst out laughing.

Pointing to the bus stop opposite, he said.

"Come on, let's get back home to the den, and I'll tell you a story. I'm getting parched and could do with a sip of me 'ome brew". he said, and holding on to my arm, we went over and caught the next bus back to his house. Grumps was quite spritely for his age, but he appreciated a bit of support when crossing busy roads.

It was a bright spring day and had been very warm for the time of year, with people wearing short sleeves and gathering in the parks and gardens.

With some folks having picnics outside, it could just as well have been summer.

Luckily, the brambles in his garden had not yet taken hold.

This meant a painless walk down to his den, which looked as shabby as ever from the outside, but I knew it was different on the inside.

"Pick me out a few dry twigs and I'll get the woodstove going," Grumps said as he shovelled out the burnt ashes. Ten minutes later, we were warming ourselves by the fire and enjoying a glass of his 'omemade beer. The ritual was not complete without him lighting up a pipe full of his aromatic tobacco.

I had never smoked nor had I the inclination to, but I could sit and enjoy the aroma as it filled the den, sweet and fruity, and it was the only place he was allowed to smoke by my Gran.

Grumps told me what he knew about the burying situation.

"Getting back to your question, it's a good one and I'm sorry about my little joke."

Grumps would often tease me, and I did not mind a bit. It was good to hear him laughing and enjoying life. He talked in an amusing but educative way, between puffs on his pipe.

"A lot of folks like to think of their dead loved ones as sleeping or gone to rest, so lying down would be more natural to them."

"Then we had the big diseases that wiped out so many, like the Plague, where people needed to be buried at least six feet deep to avoid infecting others, this would have been impossible if they had been upright, so there are a couple of reasons they bury them as they do."

That sounded quite reasonable to me, and I felt satisfied with my answer.

Grumps had not let me down. He then asked if I wanted to hear a tragic but somewhat comical story, seeing as we had been discussing the dead, about the demise of one of his old friends. I thought it might be interesting, and I loved to hear him telling stories. So, he began.

"The problems began some years back between a couple of friends of mine, Jack and Les; they were part of an extended family, with relations all over the place, some I wouldn't recognise if I bumped into them in the street.

Both Jack and Les owned enormous properties, bigger than the other family members so they would take it in turns to host these occasions, which ranged from birthdays, marriages, christenings and, quite often, religious festivals.

I never took to all that religious stuff, but if there were some free beers or a bit of knees up, I'd get m'self along there, as I did this last weekend."

"It was rare if a weekend passed without something going on. On the face of it, this arrangement worked out quite well except that the rivalry between the brothers could sometimes get out of hand."

"Like a bit of rough stuff?" I asked.
"No, not like that, but if Jack bought cheap Prosecco, then at the next party, Les would buy expensive Champagne.
If Les cooked beef sausages on the B.B.Q. then Jack would look for handmade venison sausages for his party. They would go to great lengths to outdo each other; even for the decorations, they would buy more and more exotic and colourful bunting and balloons."

"One time, for a child's birthday Jack came in riding in on a horse dressed as a cowboy for effect, of course, this prompted Les to go one better, and at a Christmas party the following year Les came in on a donkey like one of the Three Wise Men".

"Sometimes it was comical and other times it was embarrassing to see them always in battle mode.
As the years went on, things got sillier, bigger, longer, more expensive and more vulgar to the point that the younger members would hesitate to turn up, not knowing what to expect."

"Then last weekend things got *really* silly, and the poo hit the fan, so to speak."

Grumps stopped to fill his pipe, lubricated his mouth with some beer, and continued the story.

"It all started when Jack arranged a joint home-coming party for three of the grandchildren and their girlfriends, all in their early twenties."

"They had been on a 'gap year' from Uni to India, and Jack wanted to do something special for them.

The garden was lit up with floodlights and fancy candle lanterns; the patio was set up for eating and decked out with streamers and balloons, it certainly looked like a lot of effort had gone into the planning.

As the guests came in, a string quartet playing in the corner to greet them. They were playing Ode to Joy, badly I recall, and of course, the sound of the traffic and the guest's excited voices made it sound even worse; nevertheless, Jack was looking smug and pleased with himself, and he had been lucky with the fine weather."

"He'd tried to play the perfect host, of course, all the time mingling and greeting, but he found it odd that the 'Gappers' as he called them would only drink fruit juice, 'perhaps they were saving themselves for later' I overheard him say to his wife Judy."

“After a time, with the guests and family mingling and exchanging stories, Jack asked for the music to stop so that he could call everyone up to the table, then tapping on a glass with a knife in the time-honoured fashion, he signalled that food was going to be served, and ‘would you all please take your places at the table, thank you.’

“None of the guests seemed to be in a hurry to find their places but eventually did so after several squabbles about where they were supposed to sit. You see, Jack wanted to be in charge all the time, so he was trying to direct them to where he thought they should be. This irritated some, and neither was it appreciated by the more senior guests. I sat at one end of the table, trying to keep out of the way.”

“Once they were all seated, Jack announced that ‘dinner is served’ and wheeled out a large serving trolley from the kitchen.”

“On the trolley was an enormous roast turkey, and around this, there were candles and decorations. The turkey must have weighed at least 20 kg, so big that Jack could only just see over the top of it as he wheeled it along, but he had the biggest grin on his face and looked very proud and a little smug.”

“Stopping a couple of metres away from the table, he began his speech.”

‘Brothers and sisters, children and grandchildren, nephews and nieces, and not forgetting girlfriends, boyfriends and all, I have prepared, along with my lovely wife Judy, a sumptuous feast to celebrate your homecoming.'

Everyone gave a gasp and he continued.

"This huge roast turkey is, in fact, a three-bird roast.

We stuffed it with a chicken which is stuffed with pheasant, then filled with my famous savoury stuffing made from freshly ground mixed nuts, breadcrumbs and herbs, all held together with a thick full cream sauce.' He paused to take a breath.

'On the outside, are rashers of smoked bacon surrounded by pigs in blankets.' He announced looking even more smug.

"The rich aroma of the different meats and condiments drifted across the patio, leaving no doubt that this was indeed a mighty feast. Nobody said a thing, but they all exchanged nervous glances while Jack continued with his speech."

'Roast potatoes cooked in goose fat, and to finish, we will indulge ourselves with a chocolate dessert that we call heart failure.'

"The horrified look on everyone's faces was a picture, but Jack seemed to be oblivious to it, and I thought nothing of it at the time. So, ignoring them, he carved the turkey."

"Jack then started filling plates to overflowing and offered them around starting with the nearest guest, a girl called Carol. She told him she was vegetarian, and on hearing that Jack rolled his eyes toward heaven and said in a mocking voice.

'There's always one, isn't there?' looking around for approval, but nobody seemed to find that amusing.

He gestured to the other guests to offer up their plates and one by one they came back with replies like.

'Sorry, I can't eat any wheat. It bloats me out.'

'And nothing with milk in it, lactose intolerant,' said another.

'I'm very fussy about animal welfare. Was it hand reared? If not, I won't have any. Thanks anyway.'

"Everyone had something that stopped them from eating the meal, nut allergies, chocolate allergy, something, all of them, one even said."

'I'd love to, but I am on a diet.'

"This enraged Jack further and, looking for support again, he scoffed.

'Diet! Are you serious? Look at her, there's no fat on her. I'd say she needs a good meal?'

Carol tried to explain, saying.

'We've been eating differently in India, following

a healthier regime, taking advice from Ayurvedic doctors. We are so sorry.'

"This was too much for Jack, who cried out, 'Why the bloody hell didn't anyone let me know? What's wrong with you lot?'
Another of the grandchildren said.

'We have been emailing pictures and a lot of information about our time in India, including news of our lifestyle changes. We've also been posting on social media sites. Did you not read any of that stuff?'

'Emails? Social media? He snapped.

'I don't use email, I can only just about turn the PC on, let alone get involved with emails.'
Carol piped up.

'Granddad, you are not stupid, you could easily learn to use email if you had a mind to, I will be happy to show you later if you would like me to?'

"But Jack was crestfallen and extremely angry, he did not want to hear any more, he was a proud man and now he felt he had been made to look foolish in front of all the guests, so storming off he pushed the trolley back into the kitchen, it went silent."

"They could hear him struggling in the kitchen and then, to their surprise and astonishment, heard him puffing and panting. He was going upstairs with the turkey! One of the girls followed him and tried to calm him down, but it was a lost cause, as he was beside himself with anger. Next thing, he appeared at the window overlooking the patio. The turkey was on the ledge and with one mad push and shouted,

'If anyone changes their mind, here it is!' Then he sent it crashing to the ground.

"Unfortunately, Les was sitting directly below; and was knocked unconscious and flattened instantly by the huge turkey which had landed on his head."

I sat in silence for a few moments while I thought about what Grumps had just told me. I was in shock. Then he asked me,

"So, what do you think of that me lad?"

"Well, I don't know what to say, but we were talking about the dead earlier, so, did he, you know, die?"

Grumps chuckled.

"No, but he was lucky. Although he had a concussion, and it hurt his pride, he'll survive."

"That's enough storytelling for one day. Are you coming in to eat? Your Gran has been preparing sandwiches for us."

"You haven't gone all veggie or allergic, have you?" He said in a mischievous tone. I told him he was not to worry as I could eat anything.

"That's good. Come on gran, bring 'em in!"

Grumps shouted out to the kitchen. Then my Gran came in with a platter that had a cover on it. Grumps lifted it off with,

"Here they are then, sandwiches made from the three-bird roast!" He exclaimed.

"You didn't think that I would leave that whacking great roast to go to waste, did you? so while they were carting Les off to the hospital, I collected it up, gave it a dust off, and we've been eating lovely sandwiches for days now, go on m'boy, tuck in."

I waited for the right moment and said,

"That's a cautionary tale, and wait for it Grumps, it's food for thought maybe." I added, and the three of us fell about laughing.

They were very nice sandwiches.

10.
The Passing of Grumps

It never occurred to me that one day, I would find myself in my grandfather Grumps' den, sitting alone in one of the dusty, leather armchairs, without having him there to talk with.

All his familiar possessions were still there, yet untouched and intact.

It was as if he had just nipped out for a minute and would soon come back in to tell me one of his stories, or to pour some homemade ale, and to stoke the pot-bellied stove again while scolding me for letting it go out.

Of course, he was only teasing me, but I'd grown so used to it that my life would never be the same.

It was I who found Grumps, he was slumped in an armchair down in the den a couple of weeks previously.

He'd been so active and appeared to be healthy for a man in his late nineties.

But on my arrival that Saturday, he failed to answer when I called his name, and I instinctively knew that something was wrong.

Coronary Thrombosis was the cause of death, although nobody had suspected anything as he never complained of feeling unwell.

My grandmother suggested I visit the den after the funeral, as it might give me some comfort.

I had spent a lot of time there with Grumps ever since I was a small child.

I would help him on Saturdays in the garden, mostly clearing brambles, but it would not be long before we found ourselves in the den. It was a good excuse to stop and chat or to taste some of the ale or wine that he'd brewed.

Those times were so rich and entertaining, and I would look forward to Saturdays throughout the week, and I was never disappointed.

The house was full of friends and family that day, all drinking a toast to Grumps, sharing expressions of grief and saying what a marvellous fellow he'd been.

All of that was true of course, but I felt that I'd known him so much more than anyone, he'd talked directly to me, knowing that I would listen and take an interest in his life, even if some tales were exaggerated or embellished beyond belief.

While the guests mourned, I sat in his den.

No, it was our den, it was a refuge for the two of us, and I will not forget that.

The stove was cold, and the radio was off, but as I

looked at the pipe rack, I fancied I could smell the fragrance of my favourite tobacco filling the air.

The weather was dry, there was no plink and plop of rain dripping from the hole in the roof as I thought about the times we had to run to take cover from the rain.

All in my imagination you might say, but I could feel his presence there, as all the artefacts were a part of him.

They were all there, and so was he.

Turning on the radio broke the silence, and I listened to a gardening programme that he would have listened to.

Then turned it off when it came to an end, thinking Grumps would have known all the answers to the questions sent in by listeners.

He would have said,

"That one's easy. Any fool would know the answer to that, call yourselves gardeners, you wouldn't know a pumpkin from a shallot."

Then he'd laugh out loud and say,

"What d'ya think of that me lad? They haven't got a clue, have they?"

And of course, I'd agree with him, but I didn't have a clue either.

But if he said it was like this or that, then he must

have been right.

Because he knew everything and had been everywhere, hadn't he?

Pouring some of his homemade beer into a plastic cup, I drank to his memory, to us, and to my grandma, who would need a lot of moral support.

Then, turning to look at his model of the Cutty Sark, I imagined myself sailing off with Grumps at the helm, while I repaired some torn rigging.

He had drawn me into so many adventures together with his stories, and I wanted more. I craved more, but now I would have to live and re-live them on my own.

That new silence could have been unbearable, but I wouldn't let it. Instead, I sat and reflected on the great times we'd shared.

While watching the friends and relations come and go at the house, I caught sight of a giant bright red poppy.

It stood firm and tall, in the centre of the wildflower patch, unwavering and proud, and it reminded me of Grumps who'd loved his garden and especially poppies, even though they tended to take over the garden.

He'd carefully remove and save the seed pods for scattering the next year, not worrying about where they'd land, just letting nature sort it out.

Watching the large flower slowly fall apart one segment at a time, made me think,

'This is not a sad thing, it is just the cycle of life and death, everything is created, lives and blossoms, then retires gracefully back into that from which it came, really quite beautiful.'

Around two years after his passing, my grandma also took ill and passed away.

Partly, I believed due to her being separated from Grumps, whom she'd been with for nearly all her adult life.

Maybe she'd died of a broken heart?

I couldn't help wondering what would become of all the stuff in the den, these personal items that would mean nothing to anyone else, least of all to people outside of the family.

There I was, alone in the den, picking up things Grumps had handled, and suddenly remembered something he'd said to me a long while ago.

"This den is my Kingdom, and if these walls could talk, what tales they'd tell eh lad? What things have they seen and heard?"

Well, the walls were talking to me on the day of the funeral, and so were all his things, re-telling his stories and I was ready to listen again and again, and I would honour his memory by coming back to just sit, and be there.

Looking up, I saw the old Pith hat, still in the same place, hanging on a nail, and remembered the story of the African Safari.

I had waited for some heroic deed on his part, but he'd teased me with the story, and he'd only bought it in the souvenir shop at the airport.

Then, on picking up the box of photos, I found the picture of Bill, the down and out whom Grumps had met on the Embankment.

The picture had shown him in uniform, back in better times before he had to live out on the streets. Had he really seen a ghost?

Then there was the list of all the dos, and don'ts, on the scrap of paper, about looking after Betty, the Old English sheepdog.

Grumps had cut her hair so that she could see, much to my astonishment.

All this stuff was of no use to anyone, but at the same time, I didn't want it thrown away.

When I went back up to the house, some of the well-meaning friends and family patted me on the shoulder, saying,

"There, there, lad, he had a good innings, don't be too sad, he's gone to a better place."

And I remember thinking,

"A better place? What place could have been better than his den?" or the garden, that's where he was happiest. But they could not have known this because apart from my grandmother, I was the only one he could or *would* speak to.

Grumps just had to have the last word though, and it turned up when the will was being read:

To my wife, I bequeath........... Etc, etc.

And to my grandson, I leave my den and everything in it, including all the stories and memories we shared.

The den shall not be dismantled or altered in any way without the express permission of my grandson.

It shall remain his to enjoy, as I suspect he will, and to remember me as Grumps, the grandfather whose Saturdays were brighter because of him.

The den was mine to enjoy, and I'd go there every time I went to visit my grandmother, right up to the day that she passed away.

After that, the house was sold, and I had to remove his things if I wanted to keep them.

I did take the pith hat, the pipe rack, the Cutty Sark model, and of course, all the memories, they were too precious to leave.

ABOUT THE AUTHOR

A retired college lecturer, I turned to creative writing late in life, and this collection of short stories was about a year in the making.
If you have enjoyed this book, please leave comments on my Facebook page: Night Owl Writers.
Thank you for buying this book.

Peter Cook-Jones

Printed in Great Britain
by Amazon

23010551R00066